# GRANDPA
## CHRISTMAS

Michael Morpurgo

Illustrated by Jim Field

EGMONT

# EGMONT

*We bring stories to life*

First published in Great Britain 2018 by Egmont UK Limited.
This edition published in 2020 by Egmont UK Limited
2 Minster Court, London EC3R 7BB
www.egmontbooks.co.uk

Text copyright © Michael Morpurgo 2018
Illustrations copyright © Jim Field 2018

Michael Morpurgo and Jim Field have asserted their moral rights.

ISBN 978 1 4052 9497 3
65510/001
Printed in China.

A CIP catalogue record for this title is available from the British Library.

*For Jonathan, Susannah and Jemima.*
*With my love.*
M.M.

*For Mum and her father, my grandpa − Da, who inspired*
*so many of these fond memories I've tried to capture.*
J.F.

Every year at Christmas, I fetch the box of Christmas tree decorations from the cupboard under the stairs. That's also where we keep the diary I wrote when I was little. On the cover, on which I had drawn dozens of daisies of all colours, I had written: Mia's Diary. Keep Out! I always take this diary out and hide it amongst the branches at the bottom of the tree. It's never that well hidden – there'd be no point. Everyone knows it's there, because it always is, and they know why it's there too, and they pile all the presents around it. Our children, the whole family, know what's kept safe inside the diary . . .

It's a letter, my grandpa's letter to me. Reading that letter aloud – after all the presents have been opened – is as much a part of our family Christmas as Christmas cake and Christmas carols. Like me, they all know parts of Grandpa's letter by heart; sometimes they even join in while I am reading it.

Here is what Grandpa wrote . . .

*To my little granddaughter, Mia,*
*from her grandpa.*

Dearest little Mia,

This Christmas, instead of a Christmas card – you'll
have plenty of those – and instead of a present –
you'll have plenty of those too, I am sending you
a letter. A letter from Grandpa. Not very exciting,
perhaps. But it'll be different at least. Scrunch it up,
if you want to, but I don't think you will.

'Scuse the wobbly writing.

Remember last week you were helping me in the vegetable garden? I had hurt my back, so you were doing the digging for me, and stopping to show me every time you found another worm. And I was telling you to be careful with them, how worms are our friends, how good they are for the soil,

how they help us grow our vegetables, and how
the blackbirds and thrushes need them too.
And you weren't in the slightest bit interested.
You were too busy giggling as you
held up each worm to show me.

I sat there watching you, pencil in hand. I was making a list of the seeds we needed for planting out the vegetable garden: broad beans (my favourite), sweetcorn (your favourite), seed potatoes (the Wilja variety, because Grandma always thought them best for baking), as well as poppy seeds and foxglove seeds (because the butterflies and bees love them).

As I watched you digging away happily with your trowel, and humming to yourself, my heart was full of love for you, Mia, and I wanted to write this letter to you because there is so much I wish for you in your life. I have loved these days when you come with me to my garden. I love above everything your delight in it all, in that wriggly worm dangling from your fingers, in that thrush you keep calling a blackbird.

Just to see you digging there in the good earth, so full of the joys of being alive, fills me with happiness and hope.

And then there was the moment you found the frog, and came running over to show me, with cupped hands. We watched him hopping away into the long grass, and you hopped back to your digging again.

Have you ever seen a picture of us, of this earth
of ours, from space, Mia?

We are a bright blue bead spinning through infinity.
A beacon of life.

But one day, if we do not care for her, this good earth
of ours will be as arid and lifeless as the moon.

The life of this world is as fragile
as you are, as I am, as trees are,
as butterflies and bees and birds
are, as worms and frogs are,
as plants are.

If I have learnt one thing for sure in my long life —
73 this year, Mia, and that's old — it is this: earth is
a living, breathing being, and we must hurt her no more.

We are using her up, fouling the air and the sea,
making a dustbin of the land, a sewer of the oceans,
a graveyard of her creatures.

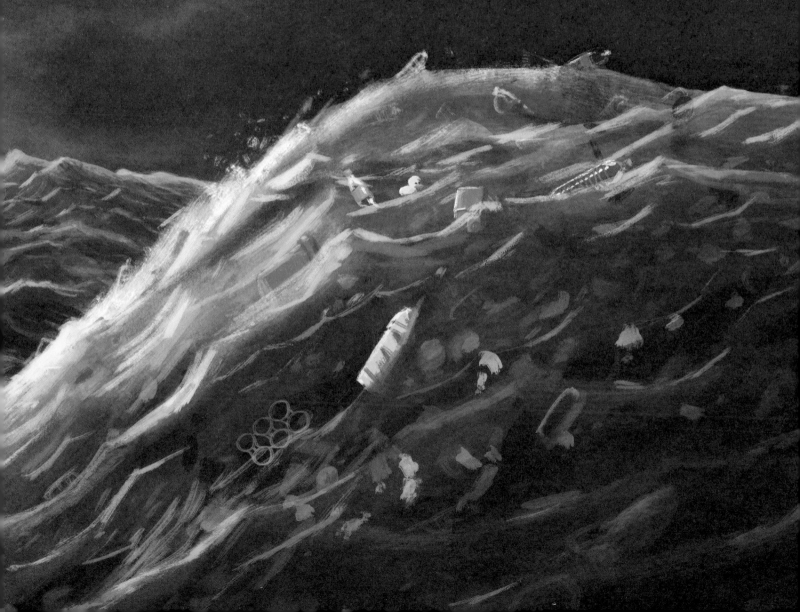

We have to learn to love our earth again, love her as much as I love you and you love me. For you and I, we are a part of this living planet, part of earth's great family. And we are her guardians too.

So I wish for you, little Mia, and for all children everywhere, a new world, without war and waste, where children like you will be able to breathe in good clean air and drink from clear bright water;

a new time when we grow and eat only what we need, no more, and learn to share all we have, so that no one anywhere goes hungry again.

I wish no tree ever to be cut down without planting three more in its place.

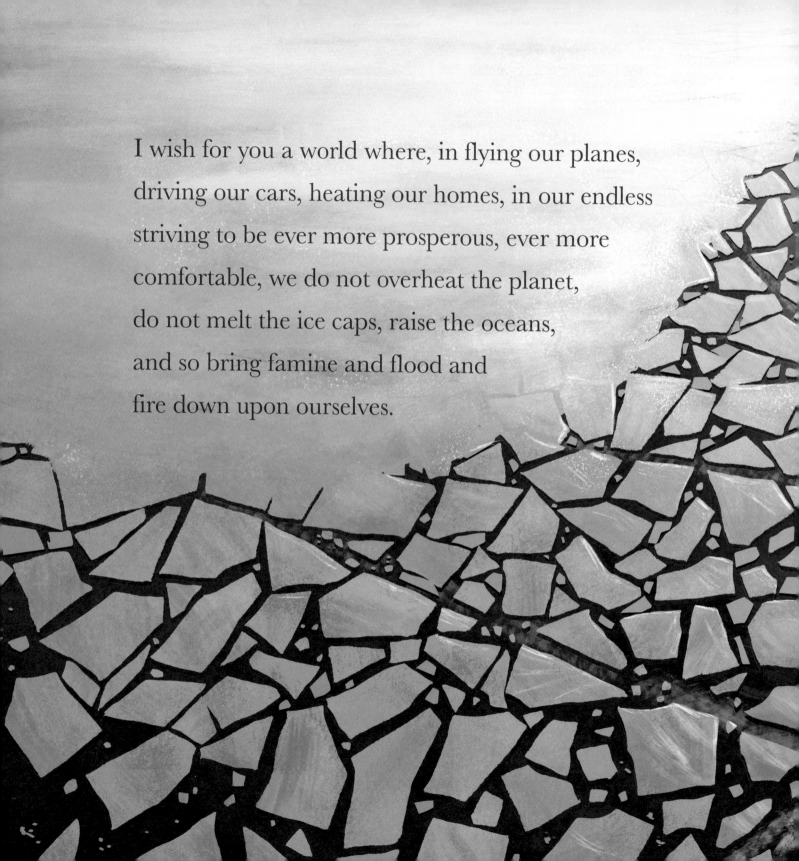

I wish for you a world where, in flying our planes,
driving our cars, heating our homes, in our endless
striving to be ever more prosperous, ever more
comfortable, we do not overheat the planet,
do not melt the ice caps, raise the oceans,
and so bring famine and flood and
fire down upon ourselves.

I wish for you a world where
the whale and the dolphin,
the turtle and the jellyfish,
can live the life of the
deep undisturbed,
in seas unpolluted.

Those same seas, dear little Mia, where we have paddled and played so often on our summer holidays, do you remember?

I wish for you a world
where the elephant and
the lion, the tiger and the
orangutan can live wild and free –
never locked up and imprisoned simply
for our entertainment, but left to themselves
in their forests, left to roam their plains and their
deserts, left to live their lives in peace.

These we have loved together, Mia: the sea, the trees, the blackbird – or the thrush, whichever you wish it to be – that wriggly worm, that jumping frog, the good soil you are digging in, the moon, the stars, our whole wonderful earth rolling through space. So, look after all we have loved together. Live always in rhythm, in harmony with this earth. Then all my wishes will come true for you, and all shall be well. But all shall be well only if we make it well, little Mia. There's a lot of healing to do, a lot of loving.

*Your grandpa*

When the reading is over, we all stand up and say, "Happy Christmas, Grandpa. Happy Christmas, everyone," and then have a family 'huddle-hug' – as we call it – arms around each other in a circle. I always like to think that Grandpa is there in the middle of that circle, with us.

It's almost as if he has become our
Grandpa Christmas.